The
LITTLE
SAIL BOAT
By LOIS LENSKI

HENRY Z. WALCK, INC.

Lithographed in the United States of America

Library of Congress Catalog Card Number: 58-12901

The Little Sail-Boat

Captain Small has a
sail-boat. He keeps it
anchored off-shore.

It is a fine day. Captain Small gets into his row-boat and rows out. He is taking his fishing-line, lunch basket and small dog, Tinker, with him.

Captain Small takes
in the oars and makes
the row-boat fast to
the mooring.

He gets aboard
the sail-boat and hoists
the sail.

He drops the mooring and the boat starts to move. Tinker sits in the bow. He likes to sail, too.

Sitting in the stern,
Captain Small takes the
tiller and puts the boat
before the wind. He sails
for some distance.

He decides to jibe ~to
turn toward the shore.
He pulls the tiller and
ducks his head to let
the sail swing over to
the other side.

Now he is sitting with his back to the wind,- or, to windward.

He comes into a quiet little cove where the fishing is good.   He drops the anchor and lowers sail.

Captain Small gets out
his fishing-line and puts
bait on the hook. He throws
it away from the boat; the
cork floats on the water.
Now he is waiting for a
nibble!

He waits...and waits...
but all the fish seem to
be somewhere else. The
sun is hot...and Captain
Small grows tired of
waiting. He falls asleep...

Suddenly a sharp tug on the line wakes him up. He pulls it in and finds a big, fat fish wiggling on the hook. He is so excited that...

He tumbles overboard!
Tinker barks! But never
mind! The water is so
nice and cool, he decides
to enjoy a good swim.

When he climbs back on
deck, he feels very hungry,
so he and Tinker eat their
lunch. The sun soon dries
his clothes.

Captain Small rests awhile and then it is time to start for home.   He hoists the sail and raises anchor.

On the way back, he
sails against the wind
in a zigzag course.

A speed-boat roars by.
The waves rock the sail-
boat and make the sails
flap. Tinker does not like it.

The sky grows dark. The waves splash over the bow. The wind blows hard. The boat heels over and almost upsets. But brave Captain Small brings it up into the wind. Then he sails safely into the bay.

Captain Small makes
the sail-boat fast to the
mooring. He and Tinker get
into the row-boat. He rows
as fast as he can to the dock.

Just as they climb out, the downpour comes. They are waiting in the boat-house until it is over.

After the storm,
Captain Small and Tinker
drive home in
the little Auto!

That night, Captain Small
has fish for supper. Tinker
has two dog biscuits.
Are they good?
Oh my!

Yes,
that's all!